SEA GULL

Sea Gull

PENELOPE FARMER

Illustrated by Ian Ribbons

HARCOURT, BRACE & WORLD, INC., NEW YORK

1

At different times Stephen had dreamed of a dog of his own, of a cat, even of a pony. But now it was something else.

"I want a parrot, Granny," he said. "Like Long John Silver, you know, in *Treasure Island*. Mummy took me to see *Treasure Island* after Christmas."

But Christmas was gone a long time ago. February had come already and almost Stephen's half-term holiday week. He had just had mumps, and so he had come from London to stay with Granny before half-term started. Altogether he was to stay with her for nearly a fortnight.

Last time he had come to the Mill House it had been summertime, and they had sat all day in the sun beside the stream because it was too hot to do anything else. But now the stream had overflowed the edges of the little stone terrace. There were no flowers out in the muddy garden. It was cold and the trees were bare.

"There're gray parrots," Granny said. "Or green ones. Which did you mean, Stephen?"

"Oh, a green one," Stephen said. "That's what Long John Silver had. It'll sit on my shoulder like his, and I'll teach it to say

'Pieces of Eight.' " He grew excited with talking and thinking about his parrot. But Granny looked at him quietly.

"Do you really want a parrot, Stephen? I've seen them restless, climbing all over the cages. Their claws scratch and rattle on the wire. They tug at the wire with their beaks. And sometimes they scream or whistle like railway trains. I think they're bored and unhappy living like that."

"Oh, I wouldn't keep my parrot in a *cage,*" Stephen said. "I wouldn't have a cage at all. Long John Silver didn't."

"Maybe he didn't," Granny said. "Maybe he didn't. Now hurry up, Stephen. You'll be eating that egg till dinnertime, I can see, and I must get on sometime."

After breakfast Stephen went to put on his boots and his windbreaker. They were in the boot-cupboard off the back room, just where he'd left them the last time he stayed with Granny. The boots had the name Alastair inside them because they'd once belonged to his older cousin. They were beginning to be too tight even for Stephen. And the windbreaker did not reach the top of his shorts. But he would never have thought of wearing anything else at the Mill House. He thought he would go on wearing them until he would have to cut bits off himself in order to get them on.

Outside, the garden smelled of earth and old leaves. It smelled of the stream, a waterweed, muddy smell. Stephen banged his booted feet on the step and took a deep breath of it because he could never smell such a smell in London.

First he went to dabble his feet in the overflowing stream. He let the water push and bubble against his rubber feet and escape quickly round his rubber toes and heels.

Then he went round the house and over the ditch into the vegetable garden. From here he could see across the water meadow to the copse where the owl lived in a hollow ivied tree.

7

He stamped his feet on the spongy lawn and watched the dent he made spring up again like a dent in a rubber mattress. He decided that he would look for the owl again this morning.

A long way beyond the copse, across fields and woods, he could see the hill. It rose above the valley as bare as a smooth dog's back. It was the shape of a crouching dog. But Stephen did not like the hill. He turned his eyes quickly away from it. It frightened him.

Although he was a town boy, he did not hate the country as some town children do. He loved the Mill House more than any-

where in the world. But even so, he preferred the kind of country that put trees and bushes and hedges round you. It felt safer and less lonely, like houses round you in a street.

So he liked the close valley where Granny lived. He liked the copse and the water meadows with their willow trees, and he loved the stream.

But the hill stood at the edge of the empty downland country. A grove of battered-looking beech trees stood at the top of it like a tuft of hair on a bald head. Otherwise there was nothing.

It was said that ancient Britons had lived up there on the top of the hill. You could still see strange humps and half-choked ditches where their fort had been. All Stephen knew about the ancient Britons was that they painted themselves blue with paint. But he could imagine them doing wild dances in that lonely beech-grove place. He could imagine their ghosts still dancing there.

He had never climbed to the top of the hill to see for himself. Granny would not walk so far, and he dared not go alone. The nearest he had ever been was to the canal that ran between the hill and the valley.

The canal, though less lonely than the hill, was lonelier than the valley. From its far bank the open downland swept straight on up to the dog-shaped hill. One year its water had frozen hard, and Stephen and some other boys had gone there day after day to skate and slide on the ice. Ever since then, even if the canal was lonely, Stephen never minded its loneliness.

But the hill seemed to him the loneliest place in the world.

2

Granny was calling from the kitchen window.

"Stephen," she called. "Stephen! Are you going for a walk? Take Dragon with you; there's a good boy. I'll let him out now."

When Stephen whistled, Dragon came bounding. He was a little, though not tiny, poodle. He was woolly as a hearthrug all over, not clipped into toy shapes like smart London poodles. He had dark brilliant eyes peering from a woolly fringe. He leaped on stiff excited legs round Stephen and barked sharp barks. He licked at the bare pink skin between Stephen's gum boots and his shorts.

His real name was not Dragon but Dragonfly, because he was just like a dragonfly, hovering a moment there, a second there, then darting swiftly off. But your tongue soon trips calling a name like Dragonfly, and so he was called Dragon for short.

Stephen tapped at Dragon's nose, and Dragon licked his tapping fingers.

"Down, Dragon, *down*, Dragon, boy," Stephen said. "Come on, we'll go to the canal. It's no good looking for an owl with you around."

There were elm trees in the first field they had to cross on their way to the canal, their bony branches full of rooks' nests, like huge, prickly fruit. Rooks cawed out of them, flapped, and settled, reminding Stephen of his parrot. Afterwards, thinking about his parrot, he scarcely noticed where he and Dragon went.

They went through the gate into a narrow path. They went past a tiny chapel, past a high green hedge and a higher red wall. Then onto a road, past cottages, into the churchyard.

But Stephen saw none of it, for he could feel a sidling parrot on his shoulders. He could feel its shifting, dancing claws.

He would teach it to say "Skull and Crossbones" as well as "Pieces of Eight," to say "Hello, Stephen" and "Hello, Granny" to surprise her. People would know him, in his school and in the streets around his home. They would call him "that boy with a parrot." Stephen wouldn't mind any more that he had no brothers and sisters.

Through the churchyard and the dark holly alley that led off it, down onto a ribbed farm track. Stephen's feet led him, but his eyes did not see.

When he came back to things outside his thinking, he saw ahead of him, much nearer, the hill. Directly ahead the road humped up to the canal bridge.

Before the steepest part of the hump, Stephen turned left and slid down the bank to the path that ran by the canal. This path was where the horses used to walk pulling the barges along the canal.

Sometimes Stephen would imagine that he was a horse pulling a barge. He would pull and strain as if the harness dragged at his back. But he did not think of that today.

Across the canal, on the lower slope of the down, they were plowing. The chalky brown furrows ran evenly, curving with the curve of the hill, running right up to where the bare hill rose. The hill was brown, too, at this time of year. It was hard to tell where the chalky brown earth ended and the dead brown grass began.

A man rode on a blue tractor, pulling the plow. Behind him a flock of white birds flew, dipping and calling, sea gulls, like white flakes, mewing like cats. Stephen loved the gulls. They

reminded him of his London street where gulls from the river
flew by. It was strange to see them here so far inland. But he
knew they liked to feed from the earth turned up by the plow.

He pretended he was a gull himself. He ran with arms out,
dipping and swaying from side to side, mewing like a cat. He ran
with the wind, and it caught his mewing from his mouth and
blew it away ahead of him.

Dragon was excited by Stephen's running. He danced ahead,
barking and trying to play, too. But Stephen cried, "Get out of
the *way*, Dragon," and went on being a sea gull.

Dragon gave up trying to play with him and ran ahead along
the overgrown path. He leaped from side to side, sniffing and
yelping at everything. When he was most excited, he jumped
right round in a circle, and he was so little and light, it looked as
if the wind caught his jumps and blew him higher.

But then, quite suddenly, he stopped. His back went stiff, his
tail, his legs. He quivered and sniffed. He barked all over again,
but a harsher, sharper bark. Something strange lay among the
grasses beside the path.

15

Stephen, still running, almost fell over him.

"Bother you, Dragon," he said crossly, and saw then what Dragon was barking at. He could hardly believe his eyes.

Gaunt dead grasses and new green grasses mingled on the bank. Among them lay a sea gull. You could see how white and round and sleek it usually was, how neat its gray wings and back.

But now one gray wing trailed at a cross angle. And blood matted the feathers on its white breast.

It had raised its head to Dragon. Its eyes were bright and angry. It stabbed its sharp, curved beak at Dragon's probing nose. Then it flopped back, overcome by its effort.

In a moment it lurched up again. Its sound wing and its head jerked and fell back.

Stephen stood looking down at it. He curled his fingers up and uncurled them again. "Poor sea gull," he thought. "I'll take it home to Granny. She can make birds better again." But at the same time he thought, "I'll take him back to London. He's my sea gull. I'll be the only boy with a sea gull."

It seemed strange that he could ever have wanted anything so ordinary as a parrot.

He bent again to pick up the bird, forgetting the vicious beak in his eagerness.

Again it jabbed out and gashed the back of Stephen's hand. "Ow!" he cried out, and jumped backwards. Luckily he had jerked away so fast that the gash was only on the surface of his hand. Even so, it hurt terribly.

"Ow!" he said again, sucking the wound. He wondered if perhaps he really wanted to own a sea gull. The blood was running down his fingers, so he tied his handkerchief round his hand to stop it.

Dragon barked and jumped, watching first Stephen, then the gull.

But Stephen remembered the books he had read about people who kept strange birds and animals. Taming them was never easy. And after all, he thought, to tame the gull would be more interesting if it wasn't too easy to do.

"I'll tame it," he thought. "I'll tame it, all by myself." He took off his windbreaker. Then he pulled his sweater off over his head and put back on his windbreaker, quickly. For a moment the wind off the hill was shivering his skin through the thin shirt he wore beneath the sweater.

This time, when the savage beak snapped out again, it bedded itself in wool. The gull's round body was between Stephen's hands, wrapped in the sweater. It heaved all of itself, desperately, and was still.

Carrying the bird as carefully as a china cup in his two hands, Stephen set off back along the towpath. Dragon ran on ahead as before. But he looked puzzled. Every now and then he stopped to look back at Stephen and to bark. At each bark the sea gull quivered in Stephen's hands. It heaved up trying to free itself.

"Quiet, gull," said Stephen gently. "We're going home to Granny. She'll make you better. And then you and I will be friends."

3

When Granny saw the gull, she said in a surprised voice, "Wherever did you find it, Stephen? I've had blackbirds and thrushes to better often enough. I even had a lapwing once. But no one has ever brought me a gull."

But before Stephen could answer, she had noticed his gashed hand and sent him off to wash it and cover the wound with a Band-Aid. When he came back, she was holding the sea gull's neck gently but firmly with one hand so that it could not use its savage beak. With the other hand she was probing its wounded wing, carefully separating its feathers with her fingers.

Her glasses had slipped to the end of her nose, and she was peering close to see.

She listened to Stephen's story, nodding from time to time. But her mind was on the bird. When he had finished, Stephen waited, more words on his tongue. He hardly dare ask his question in case the answer should be bad.

But without his saying anything Granny said, "I can mend it, Stephen, don't worry. Some wretch has been out shooting, but luckily his aim was none too good. Only two of the pellets went in and not very seriously at that. The worst is in its wing

joint—that's why the wing looks broken. But it should heal all right eventually."

Her fingers ran on gently, calming the bird. It lay panting but still. Even its beak was still, as if it knew it was no use to fight.

"Now, Stephen," she said. "I want you to help. I want you to hold its head so that it can't peck me. You'll have to hold tight, for it may get angry while I'm working. I'm bound to hurt it a bit, poor thing, not that I want to."

Stephen was pleased Granny had asked him to help her. Remembering his painful wound, he was also a little frightened that he might not hold the gull tightly and so get stabbed again. But he would not tell Granny he was frightened, though she probably guessed.

Quite quickly, when she had shown him how, he grew used to holding the gull. He had to keep his attention steady, so that when it was hurt and jerked away, he was ready to hold it more firmly. But he did not want to watch what Granny was doing with her hands. Instead, in all the moments he could, he watched her face.

He had always thought of her as very old. But now, looking so closely at her, he thought that perhaps she was not so very old after all.

Her face was netted with lines. But her hair was still black and springy with almost no gray at all. Behind her round glasses her eyes were gray. There were lights in her eyes and in her glasses, reflected from the fire, jumping as the flames jumped.

Her mouth moved, murmuring to the gull. Now and then Stephen caught the glitter of the little piece of gold on one of her teeth. When he was little, this glitter had fascinated him.

With neat, swift fingers she cleaned and dressed the wounds.

That finished, she sent Stephen to fetch a box and some hay from the garden. She laid the gull in this and put it beside the fire.

Not until then did she cease her murmuring to calm the gull, nor cease to stroke its draggled feathers with her one free hand.

"Do you know what kind of gull it is, Stephen?" she asked at last.

Stephen said, puzzled, "But I thought he was just a sea gull. I thought they were all just sea gulls, not different kinds."

Granny smiled. "Oh, no. There are a great many kinds. This is a black-headed gull."

"But he hasn't *got* a black head," Stephen said. As far as he could see, the gull's head was a shadowy brown-gray. You couldn't possibly call it black. But it was at this that Granny pointed.

"Look, Stephen, you can see its black head coming already. Later on in the spring it will look like a black hood from a distance. That's why it's called the black-headed gull. But really it will be dark brown, not black at all."

Stephen listened with half his mind. He had been too busy to think much while Granny was tending the bird. But now, looking down at it, he was thinking again. Thinking and dreaming and making more plans.

He thought of when the sea gull would be well again. He planned how he would take it to London in the train and how he would tame it and take it to school with him. He dreamed of all the other boys and the masters standing round him, admiring, and asking to hold the gull.

"What do you mean to do when the gull's better, Stephen?" Granny asked him, breaking his dreams—as if she had guessed what they were.

"I shall take him back to London," Stephen said firmly. "I shall carry him round on my shoulder just as I was going to carry my parrot. But I'm not going to have a parrot after all. I've got a sea gull instead."

Granny sighed. "You'll have to make a cage if you want to keep it, especially in London. Your mother wouldn't want it flying loose all the time. But it will hate the cage even more than a parrot would. I think it will be most unhappy in your life."

"No, he won't," said Stephen. "No, he *won't*. He'll be very happy with me. I know he will."

He turned away quickly. He went to put his boots back in the boot-cupboard and to hang up his windbreaker. He was angry with Granny. He would not think that the sea gull might not want to stay with him, and he muttered his anger into the coats.

That night he dreamed strange sea-gull dreams. First he
dreamed that the sea gull was as big as two Mill Houses. Next
he dreamed it was so small that it fitted on one of his fingernails,
while a tiny Dragon sat on another fingernail barking at him.

There was a terrible dream where the gull remained its own
size but its beak grew and grew, and Stephen could not escape
from its jabbing curve wherever he went.

But there was also a good dream, the last of all before Stephen
woke up. He dreamed he had taken the gull out in the streets
with him. It danced on his shoulder crying, "Pieces of Eight,
Pieces of Eight," and people crowded round saying, "Stephen,
Stephen, the greatest gull-trainer in the world. Come and see
Stephen and his sea gull."

4

He awoke excited and happy. Through his window the sun leaped. Even the hill looked less lonely in the distance than usual.

Dragon jumped from his basket and was excited, too, when Stephen clattered downstairs. He barked and jumped up at Stephen's knees.

Stephen squeezed tight inside the sitting-room door, shutting it quickly, so that Dragon could not follow him. He could hear Dragon, scratching and whining on the other side of the door.

A rustling noise came from the sea gull's box. Stephen rushed across to look at it. But then, when he peered into the box and saw the gull, he was disappointed.

Compared with his dream gull, it seemed small and battered-looking with its hanging wing. And it wasn't tame at all. Its eyes were quick and angry, and its beak stirred dangerously.

"There, sea gull, it's only me," said Stephen. He tried to believe it was tamer really. But deep in him he was worried and disappointed. The dream had made everything seem so easy. But he wasn't dreaming any more, and nothing looked easy at all. The thought burrowed in him like a horrid worm.

"It's not tamer; it never will be tame, not really tame."

In most other ways the sea gull was better today, quite certainly. It moved more strongly, and Granny said its wounds were healing nicely. Yesterday it had refused to eat, but now it was eager for food, gulping down bread and milk and some bits of herring that Granny had bought in the village.

With Granny it was even a little tamer. When she put the food in its box, its beak remained still, though its eyes followed everything her hands did. It let her stroke its feathers. The only time she had to make Stephen hold its head was when she wanted to examine and dress its wounds.

But with Stephen it was as fierce as ever. Granny said he moved too suddenly and sharply and startled it. She taught him to move more gently, almost flowingly like water, Stephen thought, the way she always moved herself. He tried hard to copy her, but he didn't always remember. And that day the sea gull remained his enemy.

27

The real enemies, however, were not Stephen and the sea gull but the sea gull and Dragon.

Dragon hated the gull. Granny said he was probably jealous. She said he never liked the birds she brought in, though he had been taught never to harm them.

Whenever he saw the gull's box, he went stiff all over and barked quickly, shrill, stiff barks. The sea gull's eyes grew brighter and angrier. It flashed its beak, though Dragon never dared go near enough for it to harm him. After a while Granny had to shut Dragon out of the sitting room altogether, and then he sat by the door, stiff as a sentry, barking at anyone who went in or out.

Over the next few days the gull grew better and better. It grew agile. At first it had not tried to move from its box. But one morning before breakfast, when Stephen came to look at it, there was nothing in the box but hay.

He was terrified.

"Granny!" he called. "Granny! The gull, he's gone, he's gone. He's escaped." He could not bear it. He ran to the hall door and called desperately, "Oh, Granny, come quickly, the sea gull's gone."

It never occurred to him to look and see if the windows were open or shut. He was sure the gull had escaped and he would never see it again.

He heard a door open behind him. He turned and saw Granny standing in the doorway from the kitchen. She was wiping her hands on her apron and looking quite unworried. Behind her came the crisp sound and smell of bacon cooking.

"Really, Stephen, what a noise," she said. "Have you lost a diamond and only found a pin?" She always said that to calm a fuss.

At the same moment Stephen saw something move above her head. He looked up, and there was the sea gull perched on its matchstick legs on the ledge above the door, staring at Stephen with beady, unfriendly eyes.

29

"The sea gull! There he is," he cried, jumping with relief just as if he were Dragon. "How clever of him to get there! However did he get there, Granny, with only one wing?"

At that moment, using its one good wing and its two strong legs, the sea gull did a kind of flying hop and landed on the back of an armchair. In another clumsy leap it was on the table edge. It stood there, quite still, one leg folded up, glaring at Stephen and Granny.

As still as that, you could not tell that its wing was hurt. It looked sleek and proud and beautiful. But more than anything, it looked fierce. Its pinpoint eyes were fierce, and its curved beak was fierce. It surprised Stephen who had only seen it curled up and wounded before, though he had known the fierceness of its beak.

It looked fiercer by contrast with chairs and tables. You expect to see gulls standing on rocks or cliffs or rooftops, but not on a table staring out toward a wall. It looked wrong, Stephen thought; it should see further than walls. But he pushed the thought away as soon as it came because it didn't fit his plans.

Granny said "Hm" twice, and went out into the kitchen. She came back almost immediately with a plate of herring pieces and some newspaper. She spread the newspaper thickly on the table and put the plate of herring down upon it.

The sea gull fell greedily on the herring with its curved beak. It grabbed and gulped and gobbled. It looked as if it were fighting for its food against other gulls, flapping its good wing, grabbing and squawking like a battle.

Granny looked across at Stephen. "I don't think your mother would like to see *this* in her smart sitting room, Stephen," she said.

"I shall keep it in my bedroom," said Stephen firmly. "*I* won't mind it." Just then Dragon rushed in through the open kitchen door, barking his sharpest. The gull looked up from its meal. Its beak went still. It gave a great harsh cry that made Stephen jump.

It moved its head to one side, but its eyes remained fixed on Dragon, glaring angrily, bright as needles. It looked as if it would dive down on Dragon, as if it would tear him with its cruel beak, just as it tore its food.

"No, *no*," Stephen cried. He seized Dragon and ran with him into the kitchen, banging the door shut behind him. Dragon twisted in his hands, barking back at the closed door. But Stephen would not let him go. He loved Dragon, and for a moment he hated the sea gull.

5

A few days after this the gull began to use its bad wing. It was still quite stiff, and it used it as carefully as a lame man uses his lame leg. But Granny said that soon now even that stiffness would have gone and that then he'd be able to fend for himself in the wild. But she said no more than that.

The very last morning of his holiday, Stephen came downstairs to hear a strange wild noise from the sitting room. A thudding, banging noise but at the same time soft and feathery—as if steel and bone and feathers were crashing together.

In the room the gull was beating itself against the windowpanes, first beak, then body. Tap, *thud,* tap, *thud,* tap, *thud.* Between each beat it drew back a little, paused, and then crashed again.

But the strangest thing of all was that it used its two wings equally. It took Stephen a moment to realize how strange that was. And then he found he had to think hard to remember which the bad wing had been.

Granny came running from the garden, a fat cabbage in her hands. She put it down on the table and held out her hands to the gull, making soft singing noises. The sounds were so soft

that it was hard to hear them above the bangs and thuds. But
the gull paused for longer than usual. And after flinging itself
once more against the glass, it came, blunderingly, to Granny's
hands.

She took the once-wounded wing and looked at it carefully, probing with her fingers.

"You'll do, you'll do," she said to the gull. "And you know it too, don't you, my bird? You want to be free again."

Then she looked at Stephen. But before she could say anything, Stephen said, "He's mine, I'm going to keep him. He's quite tame now after all. He'll soon get used to London, too. There are lots and lots of gulls in London."

"Free gulls," Granny said. "Wild gulls." She closed her mouth quickly, the quick light snapping on her gold tooth. She had no more to say. Instead she looked at Stephen, vaguely, gently, as if she were thinking far away from him. Her hands put the gull back in its box and picked up the cabbage by its stalk. Then she turned to go out of the room.

Stephen would have argued with her, but he knew that Granny hated proper arguments. He knew she would not argue now. She would look at him, and in the end she would win without saying a word.

So he went away out of the room also and found a strong cardboard box. He knocked holes in it for air and filled it with hay. In this he thought the gull would travel on the journey back to London. To get the box ready showed how determined he was to keep the gull, whatever Granny said.

But, after all, he did not dare show the box to Granny. He went back to the house carrying it and banged up the stairs as loudly as he could, hoping that she would come out to see.

But the door of the sitting room remained shut.

In some ways Stephen knew that the box was to show himself what he meant to do as much as to show Granny, for as the sea

gull had grown stronger day by day, he had grown less sure that he wanted to keep it. The little worm doubt had grown till it was like a great snake curled up on his mind.

It was true that the gull had grown tamer. Sometimes it would even sit on Granny's shoulder as Stephen had imagined it sitting on his. But it wasn't a comfortable sort of tameness. It looked at you with its needle eyes as if it hated you.

It was beautiful, and Stephen liked seeing and looking at it. But he didn't think he really liked it very much. He didn't like its greed and the cruel way it looked at Dragon. He didn't like its harsh ugly cries, and he was still frightened of its beak.

He didn't really want to keep it at all.

But still he hated to give up his plan. And more than anything, he felt too proud to tell Granny he had changed his mind.

6

The rest of that morning Stephen went by himself, away from Dragon and Granny and the sea gull. He went to the copse and looked hopefully for the owl. And at last, at last, just as he had wanted, the mothy owl blundered from its hole on its round-ended wings and flew silently away.

Stephen was so excited that he had almost forgotten about the sea gull. He rushed back across the water meadow and round the Mill House to tell Granny about the owl.

But when he ran in through the front door, he found her waiting in the hall. She was holding the sea gull in her hands.

Behind her the door into the back sitting room was shut, and Stephen could hear Dragon barking inside.

"Keep your windbreaker and boots on, Stephen," she said. "No, don't go into the sitting room. I don't want Dragon out."

"Why?" asked Stephen in puzzlement. "What are we going to do, Granny?"

"Never you mind," she said. "I'll tell you when we're in the garden, not before."

The gull's head swiveled round on its neck. Stephen felt that its eyes were following him as he went outside again.

In the garden the wind had grown stronger even since Stephen had come indoors. It had blown quite strongly all the morning, but now it was becoming a gale. The sky was quick and gray. In the distance the hill looked as fierce and lonely as it had ever looked.

Granny held the gull quite tightly but carefully between her hands. It lay still. Even its eyes were still.

Stephen said, "You're not going to set it free, Granny. You're not to. It's mine. I want to keep it."

But he knew that he did not really want to keep it at all.

Granny said, "I think we'll have a bargain, Stephen. I shall let it go now. If it won't go and comes back to us, then maybe it doesn't want to be free. So I'll let you take it back to London."

"Perhaps we should have some food in our hands, so that it might come." Stephen suggested. He was suddenly excited. Suppose the gull did choose to come back, he thought, though he was more than half sure it would not. Perhaps if it did, he would like to keep it after all. It was a mind-changing kind of morning with the wild wind beating at the willow trees.

The wind dragged back Granny's black hair. It puffed out Stephen's windbreaker and stirred up the feathers on the sea gull's back.

Granny said, "No, Stephen. It may come back here for food, anyway. Some birds do. But I don't mean that. It must want to come back to us, as we are, without bribes."

She opened her hands. The gull nestled freely in her two hands.

It seemed puzzled at first. It looked all round itself. It looked at Granny and then at Stephen.

Slowly it unfolded its wings and climbed up on its matchstick legs. It waited another moment. Then so easily and silently that they hardly knew what happened, it rose in the air on its two sound wings.

The next moment it stood, its wings folded flat again, on the top ridge of the Mill House roof.

Stephen held his breath. Perhaps, perhaps, it would not go. Perhaps it would stay with them. "Come back, sea gull, come *back*," beat his thoughts, willing it to stay.

The gull waited a full minute on the roof, unmoving, looking out toward the hill. Then it rose. It circled once, twice, and flew away with long, easy wing-beats, into the distance. They watched it as far as their eyes could follow. For a long moment after it was gone, they watched the sky.

Stephen burst into tears. The gull had gone, but his dreams and plans came quickly back. Now he could never be the only boy with a sea gull of his own, and it was all Granny's fault.

"You must have known it would fly away," he wept, forgetting that he had known it, too. "You must have known. It was my gull, I found him. How could you let him go?"

Granny said, "It wasn't your gull, Stephen. You can't own a gull like you can a dog or a bicycle. We made it better, and now it's flown back to where it belongs." But she sounded sad.

Stephen wasn't listening any more. He turned and dashed across the lawn and out of the side gate. Granny must have opened

the sitting-room door, because almost immediately Dragon was following him, leaping and barking excitedly, as if it were all a game.

Stephen shouted at him to go home. But when Dragon would not go the first time, he did not bother to shout again.

He had not been to the canal since the day they had found the sea gull. But he went that way now, Dragon running eagerly ahead. He did not notice what he passed any more than he had noticed it that first day, dreaming about his parrot.

When his breath could stand it, he ran. But the wind was mostly against him, and it was hard going. Often he had to stop to walk. Then Dragon would run a wild circle ahead and tear back, panting, to meet him.

Just before the canal Stephen began to run again. He ran

gasping over the steep hump and gasped at the wind that hit him there. But he went on running, even though on that rising track with the wind against him it was slower to run than to go at a steady walk. Around him lay the plowed land, and ahead was the hill itself. Both earth and hill looked almost black today.

He passed the barn halfway up the lower, gentler slope. He was walking now, panting, with Dragon panting at his heels. The earth was still plowed on either side of the track, but two hundred yards ahead was the pale trackless grass that covered the hill itself.

The hill rose steeply now to its clump of beech trees. Stephen had never been so close to them before. He could see their crests rocking wildly in the great wind.

The clouds tore across the sky, almost as fast as airplanes. But here, sheltered by the hill, Stephen could hardly feel the wind at all.

He climbed on. For some strange reason, he was determined to climb to the top of the hill. He was not frightened at all.

He had left the track behind him. He was climbing on the tough, springy grass. The steepness of the hill made his legs ache terribly, and that ache drove away any other aches he had. Indeed he had almost

forgotten the sea gull now. He had stopped crying long ago.

He was there at last, at the top of the hill. The wind leaped at him over the crest like a wild beast, making strange, sad animal noises in the beech trees. He had thought it wild enough before, but now he could scarcely stand up against it. He felt as if wind were under his skin, right down to the bone.

He sat down in the shelter of the trees and looked back the way he had come. Dragon sat beside him. Stephen's hand could feel Dragon's panting breaths through his soft woolly coat.

It was lonely here. But it was not frightening at all. It was true you could see the humps and ditches of the old fort. But that only meant that men had lived here once. There might have been families living up here, Stephen thought. And perhaps boys of his own age. He liked the idea of that. He never thought about their ghosts dancing among the beech trees.

He would always come up here and sit under the beech trees as he sat now. He knew he would never be frightened of the hill again.

The safe valley was spread out below. It was almost like the whole world. It looked as strange and far away as the hill had looked from the valley, though it looked less lonely than the hill because you could see toy-size houses and smoke from chimneys there.

Nearer to him he could see the small, scrubby bushes that marked the line of the canal. He could see the canal's humped-up bridge. Nearer still was the plowed land curving away round the hill.

They weren't plowing today. But the blue tractor stood there, alone, and there were birds, too, feeding off the chalky earth. There were crows and rooks, quite black, and other black and white birds of some sort. And there were white birds. Sea gulls!

Suddenly Stephen realized that he had almost forgotten why

he had run away up here. He
had forgotten about the gull.

Something startled the birds.
They rose all at once in a great
cloud. The white gulls stood out
from the others, dipping and glid-
ing in the swift wind currents.
The wind blew their cries away
from Stephen, so that they seemed
to float in the wind, quite silently.

It was hard to think they could
be such cruel, greedy birds. But
it didn't matter anyway, it seemed
to Stephen. He wasn't going to
own one after all.

Suddenly he was glad his gull was free to fly with the others.
He was so glad that he wanted to jump and sing. He knew what
he had known for a long time but not wanted to know, that he
could never have tamed and kept a gull. Granny had been right
to let it go.

He wasn't sad any more. He wasn't angry with Granny. What
he felt was a kind of great wild happiness rushing round and
round in him with the wind and the air and the sky.

Dragon beside him was soft and warm and friendly. His eyes
were bright. His pink tongue was stretched right out. It almost
looked as if he were smiling.

All at once Stephen loved Dragon so much that it hurt.

47

He rubbed his curly wool and, rubbing, remembered what Granny had said—that you couldn't own a sea gull but you could own a dog. He wanted Dragon to belong to him. He wanted it desperately. But he didn't want a sea gull after all. He let Dragon's fur curl round his fingers and thought how strange it was he didn't even want a parrot.

Then he realized how hungry he was, roaringly, ravenously hungry. After all it was long past dinnertime and he'd run a long way and had a hard climb up the hill. He hoped Granny would have steak and kidney pie. She usually did on his last day's stay.

He climbed to his feet, into the great wind. With Dragon following, he let himself go with the wind, running with the wind. Shouting with happiness he ran, arms out, careering down the hill, past the tractor and the floating gulls, to Granny and the Mill House and to dinner.